Notes to Parents and Teachers:

As a child becomes more familiar reading books, it is important for them to rely on and use reading strategies more independently to help figure out words they do not know.

REMEMBER: PRAISE IS A GREAT MOTIVATOR!

Here are some praise points for beginning readers:
• I saw you get your mouth ready to say the first letter of that word.
• I like the way you used the picture to help you figure out that word.
• I noticed that you saw some sight words you knew how to read!

Book Ends for the Reader!

Here are some reminders before reading the text:

• Point to each word you read to make it match what you say.

• Use the picture for help.

• Look at and say the first letter sound of the word.

• Look for sight words that you know how to read in the story.

• Think about the story to see what word might make sense.

Words to Know Before You Read

best

down

hall

hands

line

mine

rhyme

side

wall

The Line Rhyme

A Story About Learning New Routines

By Alisha Gabriel   Illustrated by John Joseph

Line up, class. It's recess time.

Let's all say the school line rhyme!

Hands are down and by my side.

I will hold my words inside.

When we're walking in a line,

do your best. I'll do mine.

Someone runs and breaks the line.

Miss Vee holds a red stop sign.

Some kids talk. Some touch the wall.

They forget we're in the hall.

Miss Vee stops and shakes her head.
"Please remember what I said!

Other classes should not hear when our class is walking near."

On the playground we can run!

We can play and have some fun.

It's time to listen once again.

We line up and count to ten.

Hands are down and by my side.
I will hold my words inside.

When we're walking in a line,
do your best. I'll do mine.

Book Ends for the Reader

I know...

1. What does the class chant before going to recess?
2. Where are the students supposed to keep their hands while walking in line?
3. What happens when someone runs and breaks the line?

I think...

1. Why does Miss Vee hold up a stop sign?
2. Why do students need to walk in a line at school?
3. Why is it okay to be loud at recess but not in the school hallways?

Book Ends for the Reader

What happened in this book?

Look at each picture and talk about what happened in the story.

About the Author

Alisha Gabriel is an author and a teacher. She loves it when her students walk in a nice line. Sometimes her sentences seem to rhyme. Her students tell her all the time!

About the Illustrator

John Joseph's passion for art appeared at an early age, while living in Orlando, Florida. As a young boy, he was inspired by the many trips to visit the animation studios just down the road at the happiest place on Earth.

Library of Congress PCN Data

The Line Rhyme (A Story About Learning New Routines) / Alisha Gabriel
(Playing and Learning Together)
ISBN 978-1-73160-588-7 (hard cover)(alk. paper)
ISBN 978-1-73160-424-8 (soft cover)
ISBN 978-1-73160-641-9 (e-Book)
ISBN 978-1-73160-661-7 (ePub)
Library of Congress Control Number: 2018967561

Rourke Educational Media
Printed in the United States of America
01-2062211937

www.rourkeeducationalmedia.com

Edited by: Kim Thompson
Layout by: Kathy Walsh
Cover and interior illustrations by: John Joseph